Earth's Youngest Explorers Discover the Galaxy

ROCKET
KIDS

Adventure to Mars

Lizzie Lipman

CHAPTER 1

Neil felt his seat begin to shake as the butterflies in his stomach grew stronger. His heart began to pound in his chest. The entire cabin of the spacecraft was rattling like a giant earthquake as the main engines ignited, preparing for liftoff. Neil looked over at Kate, his partner on this historic mission to Mars. She quickly gave him a thumbs up and a smile. This was really happening. Neil took one last deep breath. 5....4....3....2....1....0.... blast off!

Neil and Kate were thrown back in their seats by the power of the solid rocket boosters firing at full throttle. The spacecraft, surrounded by giant flames and huge billows of smoke, started to lift off the ground. Within seconds, it was soaring through the lower atmosphere faster than the speed of sound, leaving behind everything Neil and Kate had ever known, as their journey into space began.

Being the first humans to visit Mars was not the only reason Neil and Kate would be making history on this mission. They were also seconds away from being the first kids to travel into space. NASA had spent years searching for just the right people for this mission. Their search for two people that were smart enough, driven enough, and brave enough to take the first flight to Mars was a challenge on its own, but they also needed two people that were small enough to fit inside NASA's new ultra-lightweight, hypersonic rocket designed to reach Mars in record speed.

After an exhaustive search, NASA couldn't find any adults that fit their criteria, so they expanded their focus to include kids. NASA first discovered Neil at a national science fair where he was presenting his project on the gravitational waves of black holes. NASA was amazed by Neil's vast knowledge of astronomy at such a young age, and they knew instantly that he would be a top candidate for this mission.

Kate, on the other hand, had been on NASA's radar for a while. She made history a few years earlier as the youngest person to pilot a plane around the world. Her understanding of aviation and bravery were unmatched by any other candidate NASA had found.

With their combined skills, Neil and Kate were NASA's dream team for this historic mission, but it took years of intensive training to prepare them for what was about to come.

The blue sky faded to black as Neil and Kate started to feel an extreme pressure pushing on their chests, like a gorilla sitting on top of them, signaling that they were in the final minute of the initial launch stage. The spacecraft was now accelerating to over 19,000 miles per hour.

After one final blast from the remaining three rocket boosters, everything went still. The rattling of the flight deck was now quiet, the pressure on their chests had disappeared, and relief poured over them as they were now weightless under their seatbelts. The mental and physical pressure they had both been feeling only moments earlier was gone as they were now successfully on their trajectory to Mars.

Cheering boomed through their headsets from everyone back at NASA Mission Control. History had been made. Neil and Kate were officially the first kids to travel into space.

"Congratulations, Neil and Kate! You have made history as the youngest people to go into space," said Holly, the mission's flight director. Neil and Kate could barely hear her over the roaring applause in the background. "Now, relax and enjoy the ride. We'll check back in with you after you've had a chance to settle in."

Neil looked at Kate. "Well, what should we do now?"

CHAPTER 2

"Let's fly!" Kate responded without missing a beat. Kate unbuckled herself from her seat and started to rise up in the air. "This is so crazy, I'm floating!" She bounced her way out of the flight deck before Neil could even respond. He unbuckled his own seatbelt slowly but couldn't move as quickly as Kate. He was too nervous about bumping into any of the flight controls.

"Since this is our home for the next 40 million miles, I guess I have some time to get used to this," Neil thought to himself.

Kate floated straight over to the kitchen. "I'm hungry. Let's see what we've got to eat!" Kate pulled out a bag of freeze dried food. "Mac 'n cheese! My favorite!" Kate exclaimed. By the time Neil had made his way over to the kitchen, Kate was already using the hot water injector to rehydrate their food. "It's so weird to finally be making food in space after going through it in training so many times," said Kate.

Kate filled up the bag of mac n' cheese with hot water and set it down on the table. As she turned to look for some powdered juice, Neil shouted. "Kate, turn around! The mac n' cheese is getting away!" Kate turned around and saw her dinner floating in the air.

"Stop, pasta! You can't get away from me!" Kate exclaimed and grabbed the bag of food before it floated down the corridor. "Nice one!" Neil said, impressed with how quickly she was able to move.

"I'll get the juice. You hold on to our dinner," Neil said. Neil pulled out two containers of apple juice powder from the drink compartment and added water to both. As he handed Kate her drink, he accidentally squeezed the pouch too hard. Juice came blobbing out. Big blobs of juice were now floating all around them.

"Oh fun!" Kate said. She started eating the blobs that were floating around her head. They looked like tiny jellyfish swimming through the air. Neil opened his mouth to catch one, but it crashed into his nose, quickly turning into little beads before floating away again. The two of them swam around the kitchen catching as many of the blobs that they could before they were sucked up by the air conditioning system and filtered back into their water supply. It seemed safe to say that eating would be one of their favorite ways to spend time on this mission.

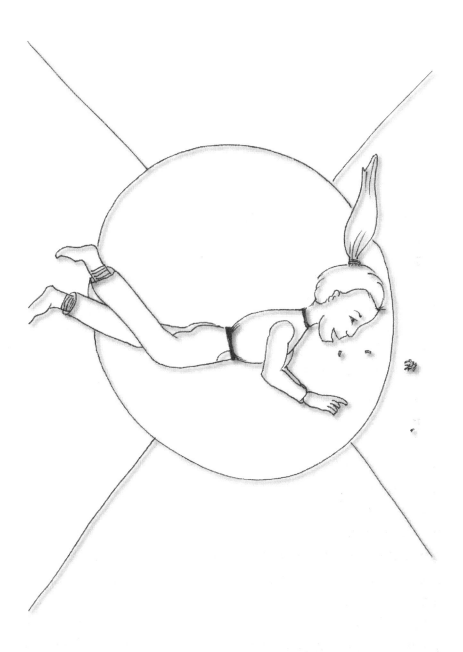

Neil and Kate were starting to settle in and relax, while enjoying their rehydrated mac n' cheese. "Have you ever thought about the chances of us finding some sign of life on Mars?" Neil asked. "Of course!" Kate replied. "How cool would it be if we were not only the first kids in space and the first people to walk on Mars, but also the first to discover life? I think about it all the time!"

"I had a dream the other night that we ran into a Martian," Neil said. The truth was, however, that it wasn't just one dream. The Martian kept showing up in his dreams for the last few months. He knew that scientists had been hoping to find a microscopic organism on Mars, or maybe a fossil of a plant, but not a living, breathing, moving being. Nonetheless, it still crept into his dreams. "I know it's impossible," Neil continued, "but I have to say, if it were possible, it would be awesome to find something like that!"

"Yeah, that would blow all other scientific discoveries out of the water for sure," said Kate. She had never actually thought about finding intelligent life in space before, but it was kind of fun to pretend for a while.

"How long do you think it will take us to get used to living without gravity?" Kate asked. "I think it's going to take me a lot longer than you. You seem to already have it down," Neil responded.

Within a few days both Neil and Kate had gotten used to their new life in space. Even though Neil kept bumping into walls and Kate seemed to always be chasing down her fork or toothbrush, their day-to-day routines started to feel normal.

One of their favorite things to do every day was to look through their telescope at Earth and Mars, Earth growing smaller and smaller and Mars growing bigger and bigger, until one day they found themselves entering Mars' orbit. They were about to make history again.

CHAPTER 3

Their spacecraft was now so close to Mars that it was all Neil and Kate could see when they looked out the window. It was a new day on Mars, as the Sun rose on the Red Planet. Everywhere their eyes scanned was barren and dusty. The thick hazy air was a reminder of the dangers they were about to face.

Anytime Neil and Kate were outside on Mars, they would have to protect themselves from many different environmental threats. Mars did not have a magnetic field surrounding the planet so, unlike Earth, there would be nothing to deflect the deadly solar winds. Also, the air on Mars contained too much carbon dioxide for humans to breathe, and the average temperature on the planet was -80 degrees Fahrenheit. Their spacesuits would be the only thing keeping Neil and Kate alive when they were outside.

These were not the only threats they would face, however. There were also severe dust storms that could pop up without warning and last for days at a time, as well as marsquakes and swirling dust tornados that could damage their equipment. However, they had trained for these scenarios, and they were ready.

Neil followed Kate into the flight deck where they buckled themselves back in for the first time since launch day. Looking out the window, they saw tall mountains and deep valleys passing beneath them. All the volcanoes and seabeds looked frozen in time under a blanket of dust.

Soon, their landing spot came into view, a wide open area of solid flat ground. Seemingly, this would be an easy landing, but with Mars' extremely thin atmosphere, Neil and Kate's spacecraft would not be able to slow down naturally from atmospheric drag like on Earth, and because of that, they had to greatly reduce their speed using reverse thrusters and parachutes. Any accident, even a small one, could cause enough damage to their spacecraft to leave them stranded on Mars forever.

Neil was focusing on their landing site, when something caught his eye. "Was that a dust storm kicking up?" Neil thought to himself. He looked over at Kate who was still staring forward. Neil quickly scanned the area, but everything looked calm. Neil went back to focusing on his landing point, but as soon as he did, a movement caught his eye again.

"Kate, do you see anything moving out there?" Neil finally asked cautiously, worried she might think he was crazy. "No, everything looks normal to me. What are you seeing?" Kate asked.

"It was kind of like a light moving. It's hard to explain, really," answered Neil.

"I bet it was just a reflection from our spacecraft or the light and shadows changing as we fly over," Kate paused, "or maybe it was a Martian?"

Holly's voice from Mission Control came in over the radio, "It could be a piece of equipment reflecting sunlight. One of the robots may have left something behind from one of our previous missions. We have used this landing site several times before for the robots that built the protective structure that your rover is parked in. When you land, you can take a look around and see what you find," Holly instructed.

On the descent, Neil and Kate felt themselves being pushed down into their seats as the engines fired up again. The spacecraft was reducing its speed by firing its engines in reverse. After a few seconds, there was a strong jolt, letting them know the parachute had deployed, causing their spacecraft to rapidly slow down as it approached the ground. Finally, it lowered to the surface with a soft thud. They had landed on Mars!

"We have touchdown!" Kate reported back to Mission Control. She could hear thunderous cheers over the radio. History had been made again. This was one of the biggest challenges they planned to face during this mission, and they had accomplished it with perfection.

As the dust settled around them, Neil and Kate unbuckled themselves from their seats. It felt very strange to walk on the floor again. This was the first time in months that gravity pulled down on their bodies, but it was noticeably less than on Earth. What would have weighed 100 pounds on Earth, only weighed 38 pounds on Mars.

The time had come to put on their spacesuits for the first human steps on Mars. They had rehearsed this moment over and over back at NASA with every step mapped out. The atmosphere and elements on the other side of the door were going to be harsh and dangerous. They had to be extremely careful because there was little room for a mistake.

After getting all of their gear on and running over their checklists, they checked in with Mission Control. "Neil and I have checked our systems, and we are ready to begin our Mars walk," Kate reported.

"Cameras and sound are working," Holly announced. "We can see and hear you perfectly. You are cleared to exit the spacecraft."

Together, Neil and Kate walked over to the door and gave each other a thumbs up. Kate unlocked the door and pushed it open, revealing Mars' cold and barren landscape. Looking down at the red dirt below them, they grasped hands and stepped down onto the Martian ground, leaving the very first human footprints on Mars.

CHAPTER 4

"What would have been a big step for a man was indeed a giant leap for kids," Neil radioed back to Mission Control. Kate was impressed by Neil's cleverness. Neil knew that this was a big moment. He had spent months thinking about what to say, but his mind always went back to Neil Armstrong.

When Neil Armstrong first stepped on the moon, he said, "That is one small step for man, one giant leap for mankind." Neil believed those words were so profound and perfect, it was hard to come up with anything better.

"You two have just accomplished something that the entire world has been working toward for decades. While your footprints on Mars will soon fade, the steps you just took will be remembered forever. Congratulations! I couldn't be more proud of you," Holly said over the radio.

"Alright," Holly continued, "it's time for the real work to begin. Are you ready to get the rover out for a drive? We just ran a full diagnostic check on the rover, and it's ready for you to get to work right away. Remember, there is no time to waste. The distance between Earth and Mars is getting longer by the day, so we need to get you on your way back as soon as possible. One other reminder. You should turn off your long distance radios to conserve power, but you can turn them back on whenever you need to speak with us."

Neil and Kate turned off their long distance radios and set off toward the structure that housed the rover, leaving a trail of dusty footprints behind them.

As they were walking up to the rover structure, Kate noticed a shadow move behind the building. "Could that be the same mysterious thing that Neil had spotted earlier?" Kate wondered to herself, her heart beating a little faster.

Neil walked over to the large steel door in the front of the structure, but Kate kept walking towards the back. "Hey, where are you going? I need help with this door," Neil called out to Kate.

"I just want to check out the whole structure before we go in," Kate replied. She peered around the back corner slowly, her heart now pounding in her chest. Nothing was there. "Why was I so nervous?" she thought to herself.

Kate jogged back to the front of the structure to help Neil with the door. Together, they unlocked the massive door and pulled it open. Sitting there in the darkness was a pristine rover that looked exactly like the one they had trained with back on Earth.

"She looks great!" Neil told Kate. "I think we're ready to take her out for a drive and start collecting some samples." Neil and Kate climbed into the rover and turned it on. The rover roared to life and the headlights lit up the dark structure, revealing their dusty footprints on the otherwise spotless floor. With Kate behind the wheel, they piloted the rover into the open. They were off to collect dirt samples for testing back on Earth.

Kate, still thinking about what she had seen earlier, asked Neil, "Have you thought any more about the light you noticed when we were landing?" "Yes, I can't get it out of my head. What made you bring that back up?" Neil asked.

"Well," Kate said, "I saw something too." Neil turned and looked at her, "You did?! Why didn't you say something? Everyone back at Mission Control would have taken me more seriously if you had told them you saw something too!" Neil felt relieved and frustrated all at once.

"I didn't see it until we were walking over to the rover structure, and it wasn't a light. What I saw was more like a shadow that disappeared behind the structure. I looked around back as soon as we got there, but nothing was there," Kate said. She felt so much better after telling Neil.

"If you see anything else weird, tell me right away, and I'll do the same. Once we have a better idea of what we're seeing, we can report back to Mission Control and have them help us figure it out," said Neil.

They pulled up to the first exploration site and got to work. Their first mission to gather dirt samples was to help scientists at NASA better understand how they could use the dirt on Mars for longer manned missions in the future. Among other things, this would allow them to learn if food could be grown using Martian soil.

After a long day of digging and gathering samples, Neil and Kate drove the rover back to their base to unload and store their samples. As they drove up, they noticed the spacecraft was already starting to collect red dust on its previously bright white paint. It was a reminder of just how careful they had to be about protecting their gear and tools from getting jammed or clogged with dust.

Neil and Kate finished putting the dirt samples back into the spacecraft and drove the rover back to the structure to park it for the night. Neil hopped out of the rover and pulled open the structure door.

"What in the world happened in there?" Kate exclaimed. Neil looked up and noticed Kate staring wide-eyed and open-mouthed toward the entrance of the structure.

CHAPTER 5

The once pristine inside of the structure was now covered in a chalky red dust. The floor, walls and ceiling were a dingy shade of rust. "We closed the door when we left, right?" Neil asked, suddenly feeling like he was living in one of his science fiction novels. "Yes, I think so. I mean, yes, definitely because you just opened it. I mean, you're still holding the door open," Kate stammered.

"We have to tell someone about this, right?" Neil asked.

"They are never going to believe us," replied Kate.

"What are we going to do about it, though?" Neil asked.

"We have to leave it for now. We don't have time to clean it up before nightfall. Let's be one-hundred percent sure to lock the door before we leave," Kate warned.

"I never thought I would need to lock a door on Mars!" Neil declared.

Both Neil and Kate were shaken up. This didn't make sense to them, and none of it would make sense to people 40 million miles away on Earth. They walked back to the spacecraft in an uneasy silence.

Neil's head hurt trying to find reasons for the inexplicable things that kept happening. Adding to Neil's headache was the thought that Mission Control was waiting to hear how the day went.

"Are we going to say anything?" Neil asked Kate. "What would we say? There's nothing we could say right now that would make any sense," Kate replied. "I know, you're right. Let's only talk about the mission for now," Neil said reluctantly as he picked up the radio to call Mission Control.

"It's so great to hear from you!" Holly answered the call enthusiastically. "How did the day go?"

"Everything went fine. We were able to easily drill down and obtain ground samples from Site #1," Neil said. "And we have put all the samples away here on the spacecraft, labeled and ready for testing," Kate added.

"Great to hear," Holly said. "Tomorrow should be a really exciting day. Site #2 is where we believe water is very close to the surface. The deeper you go, we are hoping the more pure water you will find. Those samples are going to be really interesting to see once you get back here. I hope you are able to relax tonight."

Neil and Kate started to hang up, happy that they didn't have to talk about any of the strange things that were happening when Holly started speaking again. "Oh, and I almost forgot to ask. How did everything look after the dust storm hit your base?"

Neil and Kate looked at each other, neither one knowing how to answer. "Um, we didn't see the dust storm, but everything was covered in dust when we got back," Neil admitted.

"Our sensors and cameras picked up on it, but it looked like it was pretty small thankfully. I'm really glad nothing was damaged," Holly said. "Well, you two have a good night!" "Goodnight," Neil and Kate said at the same time and hung up the line.

"Do you think the structure door could have blown open during the storm?" Kate asked. "I guess it's possible," Neil hesitantly replied. "Well, let's call it a night and go to bed. Hopefully tomorrow we'll find some answers to what is going on here," said Kate.

CHAPTER 6

The blue sunrise was brightening into the red light of the morning sky as Neil and Kate prepared for the new day's mission in search of water. "It's so crazy how the sunrises and sunsets are blue here instead of red like at home," Neil pointed out. "And, the days are red. It's like every day is Opposite Day!" Kate said.

They walked over to the rover structure following their footprints from the day before. "Do you think we are going to see anything else weird today?" asked Kate. Neil thought for a moment, "I feel like there's a good chance we will," he replied.

Still locked up from the day before, Neil cautiously opened the rover structure door, not sure what to expect. He slowly peered inside only to find everything exactly as they had left it, covered in dust. They climbed into the rover, with Neil behind the wheel this time. The rover roared to life, and they were on their way to find water on Mars. This was the part of the mission they were most excited about because the chances of finding signs of life were better close to water.

Soon they arrived at Site #2. The landscape looked very similar to the site the day before, but they both knew that below the surface could be an entirely different story. Scientists believed a slab of ice the size of California and Texas put together lay underneath them. Not only would the ice slab go on for miles, but it was also thought to be as thick as a 13 story building. NASA was hoping Neil and Kate would find water that humans could use in future missions to Mars.

The two worked for several hours extracting ice samples, making sure to properly label and store each one before loading them into the rover. Neil was excited to put his last ice sample in the rover. He was eager to search this area for a visible sign of life.

"I'm going to take a look around while you finish up," Neil said to Kate.

"Do you really think you'll find a fossil here?" asked Kate. "We are standing on top of water, so I think it's the best chance we've got," Neil responded.

While scientists in the laboratories back on Earth may find microscopic organisms frozen in their ice samples, which would prove life existed on Mars, Neil was hoping to find something bigger.

As soon as Kate finished up her work, she helped Neil look up and down a cliff side, gently brushing away the top layers of dirt and overturning loose rocks to see if anything looked unusual, but they didn't find anything. Neil was disappointed. After all of the research he had done on this area, he thought it could be rich in fossils. He had convinced himself that he would find at least one.

Their time ran out. They needed to get back into the protection of their rover. Neil quietly climbed in, and Kate drove them back to the structure without saying a word. When they arrived, Neil climbed out to open the door to the structure. He kept his eyes on the ground not ready to give up his search for a fossil.

Neil stood there, lost in thought while holding the door open, waiting for Kate to drive into the structure. Finally, he noticed the rover wasn't moving. Neil looked up and quickly followed Kate's gaze into the structure. As soon as Neil looked inside, his mouth fell open. The structure was clean, sparkling clean, as clean as it had been when they first arrived. All of the dust that was there when they had left was now gone. Even their dusty footprints and tire tracks had disappeared.

Neil and Kate looked at each other in disbelief. "This place was a mess when we left. How could this happen?" asked Kate. "This is starting to get really weird."

"It really is," replied Neil, "but we don't have time to figure this out now with night coming. We have to get back inside," Neil said calmly, "and we can't leave the rover outside. It could get damaged by a dust storm."

"Yeah, that or an alien might steal it," Kate said jokingly.

"Let's get back to the spacecraft and then we can talk about this. We need to make sure to lock everything up because who knows what's out here with us."

Their headlights lit up the dark structure as they drove inside, but as they turned off the rover, Neil and Kate noticed a dim light glowing in the corner. They both jumped out of the rover and ran as fast as they could out of the structure and back to their spacecraft.

CHAPTER 7

After getting out of their spacesuits, Neil and Kate met up in the kitchen area, although neither one of them was hungry. Neil was the first one to break the silence. "Maybe we are imagining things and spooking ourselves? Tell me what you think you saw, and let's see if we even saw the same thing? If you saw something different than I did, we must have imagined it." Kate nodded. "So, what do you think you saw?" Neil asked.

"All I really saw was something glowing in the corner, but before I could get a better look, you were running, and so I jumped out of the rover with you and ran. I have no idea what it was, but I didn't want to stick around to find out," Kate said.

"That's what I saw too, except I feel like I saw the form of a body, like legs and arms and eyes. But I could have made that up in my mind. I'm not sure of anything right now," Neil continued, "I think we should tell Mission Control that we saw something. We can tell them that we know it sounds strange, but we both saw it, and we can't explain it. We don't have to say the word 'alien.'"

"Okay," Kate replied. "Let's figure out what we are going to say first. We should probably make sure our stories make sense before we start trying to describe it to them."

Neil stood by the window trying to get a better idea of what happened, but when he gazed out toward the structure, he noticed the door was wide open. "Oh, man! We forgot to close the door when we ran back here. We can't leave it like that. Will you come with me to close it?" Neil asked Kate. He didn't want to be out there alone.

They put their spacesuits back on and started to head over to the structure. As they stepped out of their spacecraft, a dust tornado suddenly took shape in front of them, and it was heading straight toward the structure. "We have to get there before the tornado damages the rover!" Kate yelled. They took off running, racing the swirling tornado, but they were too slow.

Neil and Kate watched as the entire structure was engulfed by the dust tornado, but as quickly as it formed, it diminished back into nothingness, leaving the structure and everything inside covered in red dust. Neil and Kate were silent, both staring at the rover, wondering if it had been damaged.

Together, they walked up to the structure and looked inside. It didn't look too bad, mainly just dirt and dust covering everything. They climbed inside the rover and turned it on. It started right up. Both Neil and Kate breathed a sigh of relief.

They turned the rover off again and looked around the structure. "Maybe the alien will come back and clean up again?" Neil said jokingly. "I bet he only cleans up after his own messes," Kate responded.

Neil shut off the rover, and they walked out of the structure making sure to lock the door. As Neil turned to head back, something caught his eye. "Hey!" whispered Neil, crouching down. "What is it?" Kate responded, following Neil down to the ground.

When she peered up, she saw something moving by the spacecraft door. They were too far away to get a good look, but it was definitely something (or someone!) moving.

"Do you think it's an alien?" asked Neil. Suddenly, the door to their spacecraft opened. "It's going inside!" Neil whispered again. "There is an alien in our spacecraft! What should we do? We have to get over there. What if it takes something or breaks something? We could be stranded!"

"I don't think he's going to harm anything," Kate replied. "He's probably been watching us since we first landed. Let's see what he does first."

Neil and Kate kept their eyes on the door of the spacecraft. Finally, after a few minutes, they saw it open again. Neil and Kate froze as they watched the alien walk back down the spacecraft steps. "He looks sad. Maybe something's wrong," said Kate.

"He's an alien! How can you tell if he's sad? In fact, how can we even tell if 'he' is a 'he?'" Neil asked. "I don't know," replied Kate. "I can tell when my dog is sad. I guess it's just intuition. I think we should go over there and try to communicate with him."

"Are you crazy?! We don't know anything about him. He could be dangerous!" Neil exclaimed. "Exactly," replied Kate. "We don't know anything about him, and we never will if we don't try to at least communicate." Neil reluctantly agreed and replied, "Okay, but how? What do we do?"

"He's probably going to be scared of us too. I mean, we are bigger and there are two of us and only one of him," said Kate. "We should walk over there very slowly. Let's see what he does."

Neil and Kate stood up trying not to draw attention to themselves, but before they could take a step, the alien looked up.

CHAPTER 8

"What do we do now?" Neil asked calmly, although on the inside his heart was pounding. "I don't know," answered Kate. The alien stood as still as a stone.

"If he was going to hurt us, I think he would have already done something. He's just standing there," said Kate. She began walking toward the alien again. Neil, following close behind, was now able to get a better look at the creature. He was only about 3 feet tall, and his skin looked similar to a jellyfish. As they approached him, he began to blend in with the ground.

"He's like a chameleon!" Neil exclaimed. "Shhh! You're going to scare him away," said Kate. The alien still wasn't moving, he looked more like a statue than an alien at this point. Neil and Kate came to a stop about ten feet away from the alien. They were now close enough to see his three nubby fingers on each hand and his four long toes on each foot.

Kate sat down on the ground, attempting to show the alien that they weren't going to hurt him. Neil sat down next to her and whispered, "What do you think he's going to do?" Kate didn't respond. The alien slowly raised one hand up. "Maybe he's trying to say 'hello,'" Kate whispered. "Hello!" Neil called out, and the alien ran behind the spacecraft.

"You've scared him away!" exclaimed Kate. "We may never see him again!"

"Well, we've already seen more than anyone thought we would. Can you believe there isn't just life on Mars, but actually intelligent life? Nobody is going to believe this back home. I can't wait to tell everyone. This explains everything. The light, the shadow, the dusty structure, the clean structure. We weren't crazy all along! Let's go inside and call Mission Control right…" Neil stopped talking, realizing that he was alone. Kate had disappeared.

"Kate? Where did you go?" Neil called. He started looking around and saw her footprints. He followed them around to the back of their spacecraft. When he got to the other side, he saw Kate standing right in front of the alien. They were both looking down on the ground.

"Kate? Is everything okay?" Neil asked, but Kate didn't answer. "Are you okay?" Neil repeated, starting to worry.

The alien's smooth round body had begun to glow, light was radiating from somewhere deep inside of him.

Neil slowly walked up to Kate and followed her gaze down to the ground. There was a drawing in the dirt. "I think he's trying to tell us that his spacecraft is broken," Kate explained, "and he wants our help to fix it." Neil looked back at the picture on the ground, "You got all that from this drawing?" Kate nodded.

"Um, how can we help him? We don't know anything about alien technology. I bet our tools won't even work with his spacecraft," Neil said.

"Well, we've got to try. We can't just leave him here," responded Kate.

"Can you take us to your spacecraft?" Kate asked the alien. The alien just stared back. "If you want us to take a look at what is broken, you have to show us where it is." Kate was speaking slowly, but the alien didn't understand any of it. "I think you need to draw him a picture," Neil said.

Kate drew stick figures in the dirt, putting a line between those and the picture the alien had drawn, but the alien still didn't move. "I think you may need to show more detail than that," said Neil.

"This is us," Kate said pointing to herself and Neil and then pointing to the figures. Then she pretended to walk from the stick figures to the alien spacecraft drawing.

Finally, the alien started to draw in the dirt again with a nubby finger. It looked like a bunch of dots and a big curved line at the bottom. Then, the alien pointed to the dots. "Could he be talking about water?" Kate asked.

"Wait here!" said Kate, and she ran toward their spacecraft. "Don't leave me here alone with him!" Neil shouted at her. "Don't be rude, Neil!" Kate shouted back.

The alien and Neil just stood still in awkward silence. Neil started to fidget, wondering how long Kate would be gone. "So, um, how's it going?" Neil asked the alien. The alien stayed silent but his stomach began to glow again, but this time the light was blue. "Oh, you do seem sad," said Neil.

Suddenly, Kate came running back, out of breath. "Okay, I grabbed a white board so that we can communicate a little better. He seems to be good at drawing. I also grabbed a water pouch to show him and see if that's what he needs," said Kate. She seemed so ready and prepared for this situation. She handed the alien the white board and marker but he just stared at her. "I think you need to show him how to use that," said Neil.

Kate opened the marker and started to draw. She drew a cloud with raindrops falling down and a big puddle at the bottom and she made an arrow pointing to the water. Then, she took out the water pouch that she had brought and shook it. Everyone could hear the water sloshing around inside. The alien's belly began to glow a warm orange light. "I think that made him happy," said Kate.

She erased the white board and then tried to redraw what the alien had drawn in the dirt showing his broken spacecraft. The alien continued to glow orange as she drew the three of them walking to the alien's spacecraft. "My art teacher would be so proud right now," joked Kate.

The alien started walking away. "I think we should follow him," said Neil. "Let's do it," agreed Kate, so they followed the alien to a group of big boulders leaning against a cliffside.

Showing incredible strength for his small size, the alien pushed one of the boulders out of the way revealing his spacecraft. The alien's glow turned blue again. "I think you're right Kate, he's stuck here," said Neil.

Kate handed the alien the marker and white board, and this time the alien took it from her. He opened up the marker just as he had seen Kate do and began to draw. He drew his spacecraft flying through space and a planet that looked unlike anything Neil and Kate had ever seen before. The planet had clusters of islands dotting large oceans, and one very large mass of land in the middle.

"He's from another solar system! I wonder if he's from another galaxy?" Neil's excitement made the alien glow orange again. Kate was smiling too. They were hoping to find some small sign of life on Mars, and instead, they now had proof of intelligent advanced life somewhere else in the universe.

The alien pointed to the water pouch and to his spacecraft. "He needs the water for his spacecraft!" exclaimed Kate. Every time Kate was able to interpret a drawing she got more and more excited.

"It makes sense! If his water reservoir had accidentally become exposed to the atmosphere here, all the water would have immediately evaporated because the air is so thin that water can't exist in liquid form. He probably needs liquid water for his spacecraft to function. Hand him the pouch of water we have and see what he does," said Neil.

The alien took the water pouch over to his spacecraft and tried to pour it into an external tank, but he didn't know how to open the pouch's valve. "Let me help you," said Kate. She took the pouch from him and poured it into the tank, being careful not to open the valve on the pouch until it was securely in the tank. She emptied the water into the tank and closed it.

Neil and Kate looked at the alien with big smiles on their faces, but the alien's glow was returning to a shade of blue. "I thought he would be happy. Did we do something wrong?" Kate asked.

The alien reached for the white board again. He drew more drops of water. He covered the entire board with drops of water. "I think he needs more water," said Neil. "I think he needs a lot more water."

"I'm not sure we have enough to share," said Kate.

"I have an idea! We can drill some more ice and melt it for him in our kitchen," announced Neil. "Follow us!" Neil started walking toward the rover with Kate and the alien followed close behind. "He's been in our rover structure enough times that he could probably lead the way," Neil joked. Neil and Kate opened up the structure and got into the rover. The alien climbed in the back.

Underneath the glow of Mars' two moons, Deimos and Phobos, the three of them drove to Site #2 and drilled for more ice. After loading the rover full of ice, they headed back to their spacecraft. In the kitchen, they used their hot water injector to melt the ice and then poured it all into storage bags to transport to the alien's spacecraft. "I hope we have enough," Neil said.

As they poured the last few drops of water into the alien's spacecraft, the alien began to glow orange again, but this time his glow was so bright, he lit up everything around them. "I think we've done it!" exclaimed Kate.

The alien jumped into his spacecraft and turned it on. It began to hover over the ground, kicking dust up all around them before lowering back down. "Do you think something is wrong?" asked Neil. "I don't know," replied Kate.

The alien hopped out of his spacecraft and bounced over to Neil and Kate. He picked up the white board again and drew his spacecraft, but this time he drew all three of them inside. "I think he wants to take us for a ride," said Kate. "What if he wants to take us back to his planet?" asked Neil.

CHAPTER 9

The alien climbed back into his spacecraft. "Do you think he's leaving?" asked Kate, but before Neil could respond, the alien came back with some kind of device in his hands. The device opened up like a flower and projected images into the air right in front of them. Each picture was of a different place on Mars. "I think these are pictures he has taken while he's been on the planet," Neil said. "I recognize a lot of these places from my textbooks."

The alien kept flipping through pictures, until he came to one at the top of Olympus Mons, the tallest mountain in the entire solar system. "Did you go there? That's three times higher than Mount Everest," exclaimed Neil. The alien began to jump up and down and glow orange. "I think he wants to take us there. We should go with him," exclaimed Kate.

"But what if you're wrong. What if he doesn't bring us back? We don't even know if it's safe for us to be flying around in an alien's spacecraft. This seems like something Mission Control would definitely tell us not to do," Neil said, trying to convince himself that this was a bad idea, even though he really wanted to go.

"But what if I'm right," said Kate. "I was right about him being friendly."

Neil thought for a minute, and then replied nervously, "Okay, let's go." The two smiled at the alien and started walking toward his spacecraft. The alien ran ahead of them, clapping his hands together, and they climbed aboard. Neil and Kate found empty seats in the back and sat down. As soon as they strapped in, the glass dome above them lowered down, almost touching the tops of their heads. This spacecraft was much smaller than anything they had been in, and none of the controls resembled anything familiar.

The spacecraft smoothly lifted off, creating a swirling dust storm as they hovered just above the ground, and in an instant, they were soaring through the sky. Neil started to worry that this may have been a bad idea, but there was no turning back now. He closed his eyes and tightly gripped the sides of his seat.

Before Neil could take one full deep breath, he felt the spacecraft slow to a stop and touchdown on the ground. He opened his eyes, expecting to still be able to see their own spacecraft, but when he looked around, he saw nothing but the night sky. As the dome opened up, the alien hopped out in one step while Neil and Kate slowly followed. They found themselves standing safely on the summit of the giant volcano, Olympus Mons.

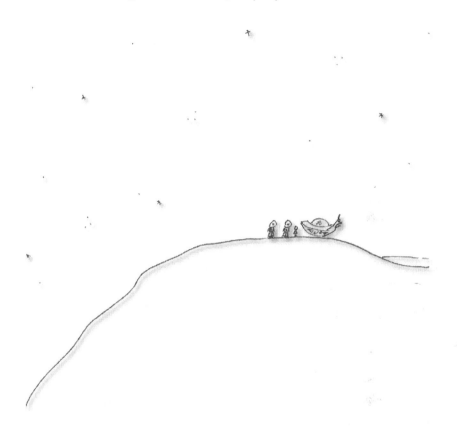

Olympus Mons itself was 374 miles across, 16 miles high and from where they were standing they could peer down into an enormous crater 80 miles wide. Everything looked so vast and open. Neil felt relieved to know he was still on Mars, but it was so different from everything they had previously seen on the planet.

Neil looked over at Kate who was staring off into the dark sky. She was so quiet and still, Neil almost thought something was wrong, but then he saw the giant smile on her face. "This is really incredible, huh?" said Kate. "I can't even put any of this into words," replied Neil. "I mean, an alien just brought us to the top of the tallest mountain in the entire solar system. This is unbelievable."

After a few minutes longer, the alien started to walk back to his spacecraft, but Neil wasn't ready to leave. This was their last night on Mars. They were going to begin the long journey back to Earth in the morning. Sadly, Neil followed the alien back to his spacecraft and climbed in. He looked back at Kate who was taking one last long look from the top of Mars before she turned and joined them.

Everyone got into their seats, and the spacecraft hovered above the ground before speeding off into the night sky. Although he still gripped the sides of his seat, Neil relaxed a little knowing that this spacecraft had to be safe enough to travel here from another solar system. "I wonder how far away the alien lives?" Neil thought to himself.

Before they knew it, the spacecraft was slowing to a stop again. Kate looked out the window expecting to see them parked next to their rover structure, but instead they were hovering above a canyon four miles deep. Suspended in midair, butterflies began to grow in Kate's stomach. They were hovering over Valles Marineris, a canyon five times longer than Earth's Grand Canyon and four times as deep.

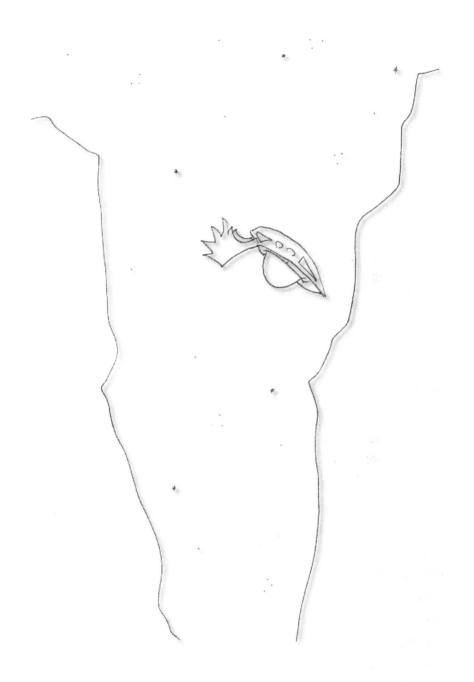

Neil and Kate were holding on to the edge of their seats, trying to steady their breathing when the spacecraft suddenly tipped forward and plunged toward the floor of the canyon. Kate started to scream, and Neil held his breath, not knowing if the spacecraft had lost control or if the alien had lost his mind.

They were heading straight toward the ground with rocky cliffs buzzing past their window. They were rapidly approaching the floor of the canyon when the spacecraft took a sharp upward turn back up the steep rocky wall of the canyon.

As soon as they cleared the top of the wall, the spacecraft did a backwards loop and plunged down into the canyon again, swooping and swerving around rocky outcroppings as it went. Before long, Neil and Kate found themselves upside down once more, pushing against the glass dome to keep themselves from falling out of their seats, and as quickly as they were upside down, they were right side up again.

The alien was glowing bright orange as he flew the spacecraft in barrel rolls down the canyon's corridor, flying three miles up one side of the canyon and rolling over to the other side and back down as if they were in a video game.

As Neil and Kate realized the alien was in complete control, and was simply showing them some fun, they were able to relax and enjoy the ride of a lifetime.

However, as the spacecraft peeked over another cliffside, the light of the blue morning sunrise was starting to appear. Neil turned to Kate, "It's already morning. We need to get back to our spacecraft to start preparing for our launch."

"How do we tell the alien that?" asked Kate. They both turned to look at the alien as the spacecraft took another nose dive down into the canyon. Neil tried to get the alien's attention. "Um, alien?" Neil asked, waiving his arm in the air.

The alien was too focused on flying to notice what was going on behind him. "We are running out of time. We can't be late or else we will miss our launch window and never get back home," Kate said to Neil. She stood up to get the alien's attention, but before she could take a step forward, the spacecraft swooped up toward the sky again throwing Kate back into her seat.

As the spacecraft leveled off again, Neil used the back of the alien's seat to pull himself forward so he could get his attention. "We have to go back!" Neil yelled, startling the alien before losing his own balance again. The alien, falling forward from his own seat, lost control of the spacecraft. They were now flying straight toward a mountain jutting out from the dusty canyon floor.

Neil and Kate started to scream as the alien gathered himself and scrambled to regain control. Just in the nick of time, the alien steered the spacecraft over the top of the mountain so closely that Neil felt like he could have reached out and touched the rocky surface.

Neil and Kate's hearts were racing as the alien slowed the spacecraft down to a hover and gently touched down on the top rim of Valles Marineris. Neil had never been so happy to be on solid ground, but the alien was sitting in his seat with his head low, glowing blue.

"You didn't do anything wrong," Kate said quietly, trying to console the alien. "It is incredible how you can fly this thing! We just have to get back home." The glass dome opened, and Neil was the first one to step out. He began to draw in the dust, hoping to explain to the alien their need to get back.

The alien understood that they wanted to go back to their spacecraft, but he did not understand why. The alien's glow remained blue.

CHAPTER 10

As Neil and Kate's mission on Mars was coming to an end, they knew it was time to say goodbye to their new friend, but Kate didn't want to end on a bad note. She motioned to the alien to follow her onto their spacecraft. The alien followed, his blue glow fading.

"Do you think we could find a way to stay in touch with him?" Neil asked as they were walking into the main corridor of their spacecraft.

"We can barely communicate face to face. How could we possibly communicate from solar system to solar system?" said Kate. Neil knew she was right, but he couldn't imagine losing touch with the alien.

Kate went to find the white board, leaving Neil alone with the alien. Desperate to communicate, Neil asked, "Where is your home?" The alien just stared back at him in silence.

Neil had an idea. "Wait, stay here!" he exclaimed, and he ran off. He returned seconds later with a picture. "This is my family," Neil said, pointing to the picture. The alien looked at the picture and began to glow orange. "We live on a planet called Earth." Neil looked around the cabin to see what could help him explain where Earth was located.

Neil saw one of the textbooks he had been using to study for the mission. Quickly, he opened it up and found a map of the solar system. He pointed to Mars on the map and then pointed out the window. Then he pointed to Earth and said, "This is our home." The alien was looking at the book, soaking in all the images.

"What are you guys doing?" asked Kate, returning with the white board and marker. "I'm trying to explain to him that we are from Earth. I think he understands!" exclaimed Neil.

They both turned to look at the alien who was slowly turning the pages of the book, as if he were reading it. Neil noticed the alien was using his photo projection device to scan some of the pages of his textbook. When the alien got to a picture of the Milky Way galaxy, he pointed to the tip of one of the arms of the galaxy. "Is that where you're from?" asked Neil. The alien glowed bright orange again and started bouncing around.

Suddenly, there was a ringing sound coming over the intercom. "That's Mission Control calling us," said Kate.

"We are running out of time if we don't want to miss our launch window."

"I wish the alien could tell us more. There are so many things I want to know!" Neil exclaimed.

"Me too, but we've got to go," said Kate. "Mission Control is waiting on us. I'm sure they are upset with us, or worried, or mad, or all of the above."

Neil took the book from the alien, and quickly flipped through the pages until he found the page that was about NASA. He pointed to a picture of the NASA building, "That's who's calling us." Neil pointed to the phone on the wall that had now stopped ringing. "That's our home."

"Let's ask him if he wants to come with us!" said Kate. She took the white board and drew a picture of their spacecraft with all three of them sitting inside pointing toward Earth. The alien looked at the white board, and his glow changed from orange back to blue. He then took the white board from Kate and began his own drawing. He drew a picture of himself with three other aliens.

"He must miss his family," said Kate. The phone began ringing again, and Neil felt a sinking feeling in his stomach. He knew it was time to say goodbye.

Kate took a turn drawing on the white board. She drew the alien in his spacecraft and Neil and Kate in their spacecraft taking off in different directions. The alien's head and shoulders drooped, and Neil and Kate both had tears welling up in their eyes.

Before leaving, the alien walked over to Neil, putting his head against Neil's. It was the first time Neil had touched the alien. He was surprisingly warm and soft. Then the alien walked over to Kate and did the same to her.

"I think this is his way of hugging us goodbye," said Kate. The alien quietly left their spacecraft with his head low and his stomach glowing blue. Neil watched him as he walked back to his own spacecraft but turned away before the alien climbed inside. Neil couldn't bear to watch him fly away.

Rejoining Kate, Neil quickly snapped out of his sadness to help prepare for their launch. There was still so much to get ready, and there would be plenty of time to think about the alien once they were safely traveling back to Earth.

Kate ran down the checklist to make sure everything was ready for launch, while Neil prepared himself to call Mission Control. "We're going to have a lot of explaining to do," Neil said to himself.

"Mission Control, this is Neil. We are preparing for takeoff," he said, trying to sound calm.

"Where have you two been?" Holly's voice sounded stressed and nervous, but surprisingly, not mad. Holly continued, "We have been trying to get in touch with you for hours. When we couldn't reach you, we started to review the camera footage from around your spacecraft and noticed some strange activity. Have you seen anything unusual?"

"I promise we will tell you everything, but we don't have enough time right now without missing our launch window," said Neil. "We've made some really amazing discoveries that we don't think you will even believe, but there just isn't enough time to tell you now."

"You're right, if you miss this launch window, the planetary alignment will be off, and you won't have enough fuel to get home. As long as you are safe, you can tell us everything later," said Holly.

"Everything is locked down and ready for takeoff," said Kate, joining Neil in the flight deck. She sat down in her seat and began the launch sequence.

Neil and Kate looked at each other with big smiles on their faces and gave each other a thumbs up. The roar of the engines shook their seats as the spacecraft prepared to launch. The countdown culminated, "6....5....4...."

All of a sudden, dust began to swirl around their spacecraft, the air was now so thick and red that Neil and Kate could barely see out their windows. It was a dust storm! "3....2....1....0...." Silence fell over the spacecraft. The engines had shut down.

CHAPTER 11

There was no jolting pressure pushing Neil and Kate back into their seats. There was no shaking, no rumbling. There was no liftoff.

"Mission Control, we have a problem," Neil reported back. "Nothing is firing, and there is a giant dust storm kicking up outside. We can't even see out the windows."

"It could take days for this dust storm to pass, and we don't have time to wait," said Holly. "The planets will not be aligned much longer. You don't have enough fuel to make it back any other way. We have to get the engines back online and get you two off that planet."

Neil and Kate left the flight deck to assess the problem with the engines, but as they were walking past a window, Kate noticed something through the blowing dust. "Neil, look! The alien is still out there."

Neil and Kate hurried to put on their spacesuits, worried the alien was going to leave before they got outside. Kate was the first one out the door with Neil following right behind. As they approached the alien, they found him projecting a picture of Earth.

"He wants to take us home!" Kate exclaimed. Neil was so happy about the idea of the alien taking them home, he could barely contain his excitement. He ran back to the flight deck to update Mission Control on their plans. "We have found a solution to get us home. There is an alien here that is going to give us a ride," Neil tried to sound steady and calm, hoping Holly would hear the confidence in his voice and just go along with it.

"Wait, what?!" Holly responded quickly. "What do you mean an alien? Like a real alien? That you've communicated with? I think we need to talk about this first. Neil, please tell me this is a joke. Neil? Hello?"

But Neil had already left knowing there was no way to explain this all to Holly, at least not right now. He ran back to the alien spacecraft and climbed inside, joining Kate and the alien.

After getting settled into his seat, Neil looked over at Kate who gave him a thumbs up and smiled. He gave her a thumbs up and smiled back. Gripping the sides of his seat, he was ready for takeoff. The alien's spacecraft lifted off the ground, hovering above Neil and Kate's broken down spacecraft, as they waved goodbye to the planet that had been their home for the last couple days, and before they knew it, they were soaring back through dark empty space at a speed neither of them could comprehend.

The ride was smooth, nothing like their own spacecraft. There was no rattling or shaking, and within seconds, the big beautiful planet of Earth came into view. Incredibly, a journey that took months in Neil and Kate's spacecraft, took only seconds in the alien's ship. They were almost home.

The light shining through the glass dome above their heads went from black to orange to blue as they entered Earth's atmosphere, and just as smoothly as they had taken off, the spacecraft slowed to a hover above a small clearing. Neil and Kate looked around trying to figure out where they had landed, as they touched down on the ground.

"Look!" Kate exclaimed. "NASA is right there! We are home!" They climbed out of the spacecraft. "Come on alien, let's introduce you to everyone back at Mission Control. They will be so excited to meet you!" Neil said, starting to walk toward NASA.

"Wait," Kate said. "He's glowing blue. I don't think he wants to come with us." She turned toward the alien, knowing this was really goodbye this time. "Will we ever see you again?"

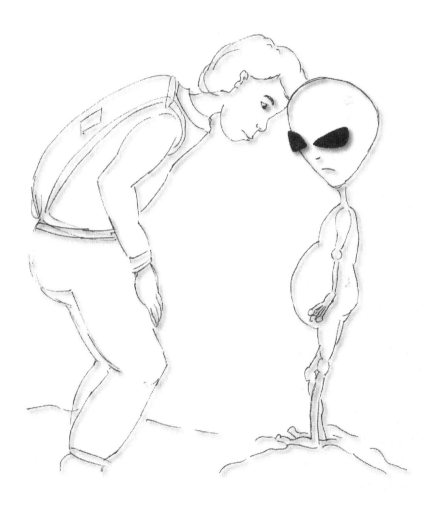

The alien's glow turned orange as he ran back to his spacecraft to grab his projector. When he came back, he projected a picture of Saturn, followed by a picture of Saturn aligned with Mars, and then a picture of NASA. "He wants to take us on another trip!" Kate said excitedly.

"Not just any trip. He wants to take us to Saturn!" Neil exclaimed. "Ok, we'll come right back to this spot when Saturn aligns with Mars. Goodbye, good friend!" Neil put his forehead on the alien's. The alien's belly began to glow orange again, but this time, the orange glow kept getting brighter and brighter until it turned into a pure white light. "See you soon," added Neil.

The alien walked over and put his head against Kate's. "Goodbye," Kate said with tears in her eyes. She gave him a big hug. "Until next time," she said.

Neil and Kate watched as the alien climbed back into his spacecraft and disappeared into the sky. "When is the next time Saturn aligns with Mars?" asked Kate.

"We'll have to look it up," replied Neil. They both stood in silence for a moment staring up at the blue sky. "Are you ready to head inside?" asked Kate.

"We are going to have a lot of explaining to do," replied Neil. "Do we ever!" said Kate. They walked into Mission Control where everyone was running around frantically.

Nobody even noticed them standing in the doorway.

Kate nervously cleared her throat. "Hi everyone," she said. The room grew silent, as everyone turned around to look at them. Neil and Kate felt like regular kids again, kids that were about to be in a lot of trouble.

Then, suddenly, the room erupted into cheers. Holly was the first one to run over to them, picking them both up in her arms and swinging them around. "We thought we had lost you, but you're here! You're home! How did you get here!?!?"

Neil and Kate's families came running over next. Everyone was crying and smiling at the same time. Neil's little brother started peppering them with questions. "How did you get back? Did you bring me anything? Did you really meet an alien?"

Giant smiles spread across Neil and Kate's faces. "You're not going to believe what happened," Neil said, "and wait until you hear where we're going next!

THE END

Made in the USA
Columbia, SC
03 November 2021

48324331R00043